GUNPOINT

GUNPOINT

JIM ELDRIDGE

With illustrations by
Dan Chernett

Barrington Stoke

For Lynne, for ever

First published in 2016 in Great Britain by
Barrington Stoke Ltd
18 Walker Street, Edinburgh, EH3 7LP

www.barringtonstoke.co.uk

A CIP catalogue record for this book is available
from the British Library upon request

ISBN: 978-1-78112-515-1

Printed in China by Leo

Contents

Chapter 1
999

Alex was cramped in the roof space of the Town Hall with her plans and her tool bag. She had just set out the water pipes when she heard the shout from below.

"Put your hands up! Stay still! If anyone moves, we shoot!"

Alex shifted the pipes to one side, went to the roof hatch and looked down.

She could see the scaffolding she and her dad had put up so they could get into the roof space to upgrade the water pipes. The room below had a very high ceiling like all the rooms in the Town Hall. It was a very old building.

Two men stood next to the scaffolding. Their faces were covered with black masks and they had lined up everyone in the room against a wall. Ten people stood with their hands up. One of them was Alex's dad! The two men were pointing guns at him and the others.

Alex moved back from the hatch into the darkness of the roof space. Her heart pounded as she took out her mobile and rang 999.

"I'm at the Town Hall in Albert Street," she whispered. "There are armed men here. They've taken ten people hostage. One of them's my dad ..."

Voices from below interrupted her and she looked down again. One of the gunmen was on his phone too.

"We're in the Town Hall and we're armed," he said. "We've got ten hostages. You've got an hour to release Ken Bull from prison. Do it now. If you don't, we start shooting. Never

mind my name – you can call me Mr Blue."

Chapter 2
Alarm

"Caller, what's your name?" the voice on the line asked.

Alex shuffled away from the hatch. "Alex Winter," she whispered into the phone. "I'm fixing pipes in the roof space. They don't know I'm here."

"How many of them are there?" the operator asked.

"Two gunmen and ten hostages," Alex told her.

There was a pause, then the operator said, "We are aware of this situation. Do nothing.

Stay where you are. The police will deal with it."

Alex knew she should follow the woman's advice. But then she heard more voices from below. She knew it was dangerous, but she moved over to look down from the hatch again. Two more men had come in from the stairs.

They had guns and there were more hostages with them. The hostages were ordinary office workers, and their faces were pale with terror. The gunmen must have rounded up everyone in the building.

And then, as Alex watched, holding her breath – her mobile rang!

"There's someone up there!" one of the gunmen shouted out in alarm. "At the top of the scaffolding!"

"No! That's my phone," Alex's dad said. "I left it up there. I'm a plumber, fixing the pipes in the roof."

Alex swore to herself – why hadn't she switched her phone to silent?

She switched it off. She couldn't afford any more mistakes like that.

Down below she could hear the guy who called himself Mr Blue talking. He seemed to be the gunmen's leader.

"Climb up and see if anyone's there," he said to one of the others.

Alex picked up a chunk of scaffolding pipe from the floor. 'When he puts his head through the hatch, I'll hit him,' she thought.

Then she realised that wasn't a good idea.
If she did that they'd all know she was up here.

She listened. The gunman was half way up
the scaffolding.

"Bring that phone down with you!" Mr Blue
shouted.

'I need to hide,' Alex thought.

She moved back into the roof space and crouched down behind a water tank.

Would the man search the roof space? If he did, he'd be sure to find her. What would he do then? Would he shoot her?

Chapter 3
Accident

Alex peeped past the water tank and a tangle of pipes towards the open hatch. A man's head appeared, the face covered by a mask. He climbed into the roof space and Alex saw the heavy black gun in his hand. He looked around, saw Alex's phone and picked it up.

"There's no one here!" he called. "I've got the phone!"

He turned his back, and Alex heard him climbing back down. She breathed a sigh of relief.

'I've got to do something,' she told herself. 'I've got to save Dad. And all those other people.'

Alex took the plan of the water system out of the pocket of her trousers and checked it.

Pipes ran from the water tank to the far end of the roof space. Then they went down a narrow gap behind the wall right down to the ground floor. At the bottom there was a small opening marked on the plan.

Alex didn't know how big the opening was, but she hoped she was small enough to squeeze into it.

Alex packed her tool bag with a heavy spanner, a screwdriver, a roll of gaffer tape and a pair of scissors. The whole time she tried not to make any noise. She also packed the plan of the building so she'd know where she was.

She heard Mr Blue talking again. He was setting out his demands to the police.

"Bring Ken Bull by helicopter to the roof of the Town Hall," he said. "We'll tell the pilot where to take us. We'll take two hostages with us, just in case. Got it?"

With her tool bag in her hand, Alex crawled to the roof hatch to take another look down. Mr Blue was still on the phone, listening. Alex's dad and the other hostages were still backed up against the wall.

All of a sudden one of the hostages made a move – a small man in the dark blue uniform of a security guard. He jumped out at one of the gunmen, grabbed his arm and twisted it up his back.

Another gunman aimed at the security
guard and fired.

BANG!

The security guard yelled out in pain and
fell to the floor.

"That was nothing!" Mr Blue shouted into the phone. "An accident. Someone did something stupid and they got shot. He's not dead. Not yet. But if you want him to live, you'd better get that helicopter here fast!"

Chapter 4
Locked

Alex was terrified by what she had seen and she shook as she crawled across the roof space. At last she got to the far side and the hole in the floor where the water pipes and electric cables went down.

Alex hung her tool bag around her neck.
Then she took hold of the pipes and lowered
herself into the hole.

It was tricky climbing down the pipes. The
tool bag was heavy against her body and the
space in the shaft was very narrow. She was

worried that the bag would swing and make a noise and the gunmen would hear her.

Alex was sweaty and shaky with effort when at last she got to the bottom. She stood there in the narrow shaft and listened. She could hear voices, but they were a good way away.

As Alex had hoped, there was a plastic grate fixed by clips. Alex needed to get through it to get out of the shaft. She opened the clips with her screwdriver and pushed the grille out. Then she slipped out through the hole and into an office on the other side.

She was still inside the building, but away from the gunmen and hostages.

She clipped the plastic grate back in place.

Now what? Alex had no idea what to do next. One thing was for sure – she couldn't

take on four armed men. The best thing would
be to find a door to the outside. The police
must be outside, watching the building. Maybe
if Alex opened a door she could let them in.

As she stood there thinking, Alex heard
heavy footsteps coming towards her.

Just in time, she slid behind a big wooden
desk and hid. One of the gunmen appeared.
He walked past the desk, went through a door,
then returned a minute later and headed back
the way he'd come.

Alex crept out from behind the desk and
followed him, staying close to the walls.

The gunman went round a corner, and she heard him say, "That door's locked as well."

Alex peered round the corner. The hostages and the gunmen were still in the same room.

She saw her dad kneel down by the security guard and put a bandage on his arm. There was a First Aid box open on the floor beside him. The security guard was sitting up, but pain had drained all the colour from his face. The other hostages stood still and silent against the wall.

"So all the doors to the outside are locked," Mr Blue said. "Good. No one can get in."

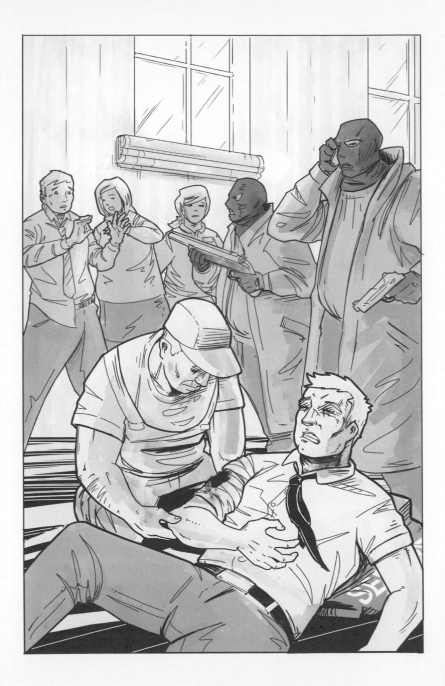

He tapped out a number on his phone.

"Where's that helicopter?" he demanded. "You've got 15 minutes. No more. If that helicopter isn't here by then, I shoot one of the hostages. And the next one won't just be hurt. They'll be dead!"

Chapter 5
Spanner

Just 15 minutes! Alex needed to act fast. She crept back the way she'd come and sneaked into her hiding place behind the desk.

If all the outside doors were locked, then she couldn't open one to let the police in.

Alex took the plan of the plumbing system out of her bag and looked at it. There was a toilet not far away and the plan showed that the toilet had a window to the outside.

But the toilet was on the other side of the door Alex had seen the gunman go through. She tiptoed out from behind the desk and went through the door. There were two more doors on the other side. One was a door to the outside with a sign on it that said, "This door must be kept locked for security reasons."

The other one was marked "Gents".

Alex went in. She saw the window, but it was bolted shut.

Alex took the spanner from her bag and began to work on the bolt. Her heart almost stopped when the door opened and one of the gunmen came in. He looked at her, his mouth in an O of shock. Then he went for his gun.

SMACK!

Alex swung the spanner hard and hit him in the face.

SMACK!

Alex flinched at the sound and the sight of the man's blood but she braced herself and hit him a third time with the spanner. This time she hit him on the head. He fell down, out cold.

Alex knew that she had to move fast before the other gunmen came looking for him. She couldn't risk it that he might get up and sound the alarm.

Alex pulled gaffer tape and scissors from her bag and stuck a strip of tape over the

gunman's mouth. Then she used some more
tape to bind his wrists together.

She pushed and shoved and pulled his body
until it was wedged against the door to stop it
opening. He was much bigger than she was and
it was hard work.

Then Alex went back to work on the window bolt with the spanner. Her hands were sweating and the bolt was stiff, but at last she began to get it loose.

But just as she thought she'd got there with the bolt, Alex heard a noise. She froze as someone pushed against the door.

"Oi, Charlie!" a voice said.

Chapter 6
Shoot

The person outside pushed again on the door, but it stayed shut, held by the gunman's body.

"Get a move on!" the voice shouted. "The boss wants us. Five minutes and he'll start shooting."

Then Alex heard footsteps walking away.

She went back to the bolt, working as fast as she could. They were going to start shooting the hostages! And one of them was her dad!

At last the bolt came free. Alex pushed open the window and was just about to climb out, when a voice snarled, "Freeze!"

A man in a balaclava and goggles was pointing a rifle at her. Other men in black body armour were behind him. It was the police – an Armed Response Unit.

"I'm just a plumber," Alex said. She pointed back into the toilet. "One of the gunmen's here. I knocked him out, but there are three other gunmen upstairs. They've got a load of hostages and they're going to start shooting them."

"Step back," the police officer ordered.

Alex moved away from the window, and six police officers crawled in the open window, one by one.

"Right," the first one said to Alex. "You climb out and run."

Alex shook her head. "No," she said. "My dad's one of the hostages. And I know where everyone is. I can take you there."

"Sorry," the man said. "We can't put you at risk like that."

Alex pointed at the gunman, who was still out cold.

"I dealt with this one on my own," she said.

"Good point," one of the officers said. "Well made."

"OK." The first officer nodded. "But you do exactly what I say."

The police officers dragged the gunman away from the door and Alex led the way out.

The first officer was right next to Alex as she led the policemen back to the big room where the gunmen and hostages were. She could hear Mr Blue on his mobile.

"Come on!" he was shouting. "You've got two minutes! Where's this helicopter? I'm not kidding when I say we'll start shooting!"

Then Alex heard him grumble to his men. "Where's Charlie? What's taking him so long?"

"Shall I go and call him again?" one of the other gunmen asked.

"No," Mr Blue said. "There's no time. If we don't shoot one soon they'll know we're bluffing. Set it up and I'll film it on my phone and send it to them. That way they'll know we mean business."

"Which one first, boss?" the gunman asked.

"The plumber," Mr Blue said. "Start with him."

Chapter 7
All Over

"No!" Alex cried, and she started to rush out towards her dad.

But before she could move, one of the officers grabbed her and threw her backwards. As she fell to the floor she saw two police officers fling something towards the gunmen

and the hostages, then dash for cover behind
the corner of a wall.

The next thing there was a frenzy of
explosions and shouting and screams. Then the
police officers rushed out from the cover of the
wall.

It was all over in minutes. One of the officers came back for Alex and took her into the big room.

The three gunmen were lying face down on the floor with their hands on the backs of their heads. Two bulky police officers stood guard over them with their rifles.

The hostages were sitting on the floor, rubbing their eyes. Alex rushed to her dad.

"Dad!" she cried and threw her arms around him.

"Alex? Is that you?" her dad asked, blinking fast. "I can't see."

"You'll be all right in a minute," one of the officers told him. "It's a stun grenade. The white light makes you blind and deaf, but only for a bit."

"What?" Alex's dad said.

"It makes you BLIND and DEAF!" the officer shouted.

Alex's dad blinked a few more times.

"I can see again," he said. "But everything looks cloudy and I still can't hear. Won't someone please explain to me what's going on?"

But then the police officers turned their attention to the other hostages. They gave the wounded security guard First Aid while they waited for an ambulance.

"It's all over, Dad," Alex said. "It's OK now."

She'd never had to look after her dad like this before. Up till now he'd always been the one to take care of her.

"I thought you were up in the roof," her dad said. His hearing had come back now.

"I was," Alex said, "but I got out down one of the pipes."

"She did a lot more than that," a voice said.

Alex and her dad looked at the Armed Response Unit commander who'd come over and was now standing beside them.

"Your daughter knocked out one of the gunmen and let us into the building," he said. "Without her bravery and quick thinking, people would have died today."

He turned to Alex and asked, "What's your name?"

"Alex Winter."

"We could use a young woman like you in the police, Alex," he said. "Have you ever thought of joining?"

Alex shook her head and grinned at him.

"No thanks," she said. "At least not just yet. I think I'll stick with being a plumber. Like my dad."

Our books are tested
for children and young people by
children and young people.

Thanks to everyone who consulted on
a manuscript for their time and effort in
helping us to make our books better
for our readers.

JIM ELDRIDGE has written lots of nail-biting adventure stories, including ...

The clock is ticking...

BOMB!

JIM ELDRIDGE

Tick ... Tick ... Tick ...

Rob's a top bomb disposal expert.

He must defuse a bomb in a school before it's too late.

The clock is ticking – can he do it?

www.barringtonstoke.co.uk

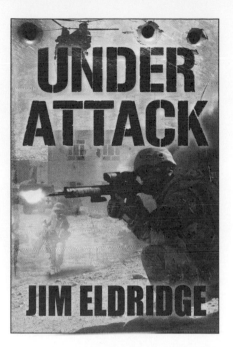

Incoming! Take cover! Dr Sari Patel and Captain
Joe MacBride are under fire!

The Taliban attack the hospital Sari and Joe are
building. A young girl is hurt by a bomb.

Joe must draw fire away from the village while
Sari performs the most dangerous operation of
her life.

Can Sari and Joe hang on in there?